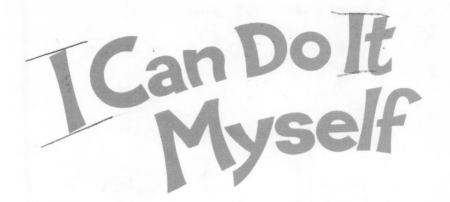

I Can Do It Myself

by Emily Perl Kingsley

Illustrated by Richard Brown

Featuring Jim Henson's Sesame Street Muppets

A SESAME STREET/GOLDEN PRESS BOOK
Published by Western Publishing Company, Inc.
in conjunction with
Children's Television Workshop.

I can put my toys away.

I can do it myself.

I can pour my juice.

I can button my buttons.

I can comb my hair.

I can water my plant.

I can put on my boots.

I can write my name.

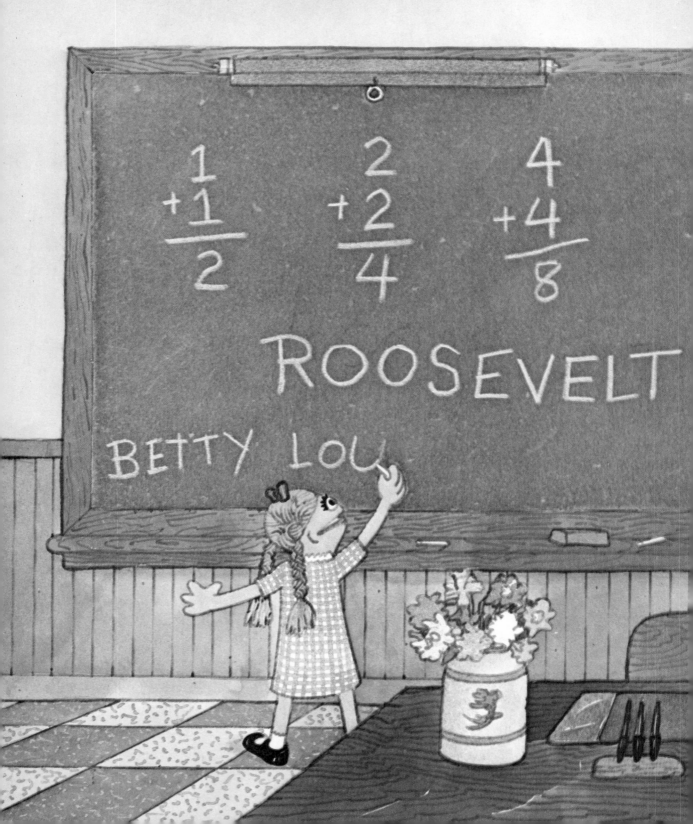

I can make my bed.

I can do it myself.

I can ride my tricycle.

I can set the table.

I can brush my teeth.

I can look at this whole book.

I can do it myself!

ABCDEFGH